6/96

ID0960363

The
HAYLOFT

The
HAYLOFT

by Lisa Westberg Peters
pictures by K. D. Plum

DIAL BOOKS FOR YOUNG READERS

NEW  YORK

Dial easy-to-read

For my daughters,
Emily and Anna

L. W. P.

For the new kids:
Sheelagh and Thomas

K. D. P.

Published by Dial Books for Young Readers
A Division of Penguin Books USA Inc.
375 Hudson Street
New York, New York 10014

The Dial Easy-to-Read logo is a registered trademark of
Dial Books for Young Readers,
A Division of Penguin Books USA Inc.,
® TM 1,162,718.

Library of Congress Cataloging in Publication Data
Peters, Lisa Westberg.
The hayloft / by Lisa Westberg Peters ; pictures by K. D. Plum.
p.   cm.
Summary: Two sisters living on a farm enjoy many summer activities—
especially spending the night in the hayloft.
ISBN 0-8037-1490-4 (tr).—ISBN 0-8037-1491-2 (lib)
[1. Sisters—Fiction.   2. Play—Fiction.   3. Farm life—Fiction.
4. Summer—Fiction.]   I. Plum, K. D., ill.   II. Title.
PZ7.P44174Hay 1995   [E]—dc20   93-18718   CIP   AC

First Edition
1 3 5 7 9 10 8 6 4 2

The art for each picture consists of pencil, dye, watercolor, and
gouache, which is scanner-separated and reproduced in full-color.

Reading Level 2.1

E
PET

CONTENTS

HERE, HEBBY!

Caroline Rose and her little sister,

Ivy, lived on a farm.

They had cows and sheep and a cat

named Hebby.

The two sisters helped to take care

of the cows and the sheep.

But Hebby took care of herself.

"I wish Hebby were a dog,"

said Ivy as she flicked

bugs off the bean blossoms

with her braids.

"We could play catch with her.

We could take her for walks."

"Hebby is a farm cat,"

said Caroline Rose

as she twisted her curls.

"Farm cats do not like

to take walks."

"I still wish she were a dog,"

said Ivy.

"Well," said Caroline Rose,

"we could *pretend* she is a dog.

Just for today."

They found a collar and a leash.

But when they tried to put it on,

Hebby ran away.

She ran around the corncrib.

But they could not catch her.

She ran up an oak tree.

But they could not climb as high.

"Here, Hebby!" they called.

"Here, Hebby!" they called again.

Hebby hurried down the tree

and disappeared.

Caroline Rose and Ivy checked

all of Hebby's favorite spots—

the basket in the toolshed,

the soft place under the rosebush,

and the welcome mat on the steps.

Hebby was not there.

14

"What if she ran away for good?"
said Ivy.

"What if she gets hurt?"
said Caroline Rose.

"What if…what if…?" said Ivy.

She tied her braids in a knot.

"We can try one more place,"
said Caroline Rose. "Follow me."

They ran across the yard to the barn.

They opened the heavy wooden door.

Squeak! They climbed the ladder

one step at a time.

Up, up, higher than the barn door.

Up, up, higher than the spiderwebs.

Up, up, plop—

onto the floor of the hayloft.

Hay was stacked high

like giant loaves of bread.

It smelled as sweet

as a field in spring.

"Woof, woof!" called Ivy.

"Bowwow!" called Caroline Rose.

She rattled the leash.

Ivy sighed. "We will never find her.

If Hebby were a dog,

we could find her.

She would be on a leash."

Caroline Rose sighed. "I know."

Suddenly a ball of gray stripes

streaked past them. It was Hebby.

She leaped over the hay bales.

She chased a mouse

across the rafters.

She poked her nose in a spiderweb.

And she batted at the dust

in a sunbeam.

Caroline Rose and Ivy

forgot about Hebby the dog.

They sat down in the hay

to watch Hebby play.

"I guess Hebby is best as a cat,"

said Ivy.

"I know," said Caroline Rose.

TOO HOT

It was a hot and sticky day.

The cows were too hot to moo.

The corn was too hot to grow.

Caroline Rose and Ivy stood

in the shade of the barn.

They wanted to swing on the rope

in the hayloft.

But they were too hot and sticky.

"I am hotter than you,"

said Caroline Rose,

"because I am bigger than you.

There is more of me to be hot."

"No," said Ivy. "I am hotter
than you because I am smaller.
The sun heats me up faster."

"That is silly," said Caroline Rose.

Ivy sighed. "What should we do?"

"I have an idea," said Caroline Rose.

"We can wade in the pond.

That will make us cool."

Caroline Rose and Ivy ran to the pond.

Ivy dipped in a toe.

It came out green.

"Ugh," said Ivy.

"The pond will not make us cool.

It will just make us green."

Caroline Rose said,

"I have another idea.

We can suck on ice cubes

from the freezer."

They climbed down the cellar stairs.

They opened the freezer.

They sucked on ice cubes.

But they were still hot.

Caroline Rose said,

"Maybe we could lie

under the apple tree.

We could pretend it is winter

and snow is falling."

29

They lay under the apple tree
and closed their eyes.

A leaf fell on Ivy.

A bug fell on Caroline Rose.

"I am still hot," said Ivy.

"I wish we had a sprinkler."

A drop fell on Ivy's nose.

A drip fell on Caroline Rose's ear.

Dark clouds were gathering

in the hot and sticky sky.

"Whoopee!" cried Ivy.

"We can play in the rain."

Lightning flashed. They blinked.

Thunder crashed. They shook.

"Get in the barn!"

shouted Caroline Rose.

Safe in the hayloft,

Caroline Rose and Ivy

watched the rain fall outside.

But they *felt* the rain

fall inside.

It dripped through the cracks

of the leaky roof.

It dripped everywhere, even on Hebby.

Caroline Rose grabbed the swing.

"Ivy! We *do* have a sprinkler!

A hayloft sprinkler!"

She swung across the barn

and bumped into cool drips one way,

cool drips the other way.

Back and forth they flew

like barn swallows for the rest

of the rain-cool day.

SLEEPING IN THE HAY

Caroline Rose and Ivy always slept

in their own room

in their own bunk beds.

One night Caroline Rose said,

"Let's sleep in the hayloft.

We have never slept there.

We can sleep with Hebby."

"Great!" said Ivy.

"And," said Caroline Rose,

"we can sleep with the spiders

and the mice and the bats."

Ivy shook her head and said,

"Maybe we should sleep

in our own room and *pretend*

we are sleeping in the hayloft."

"We will be fine," said Caroline Rose.

"If we are not fine, we can leave."

"Right away?" asked Ivy.

"Right away," said Caroline Rose.

They brought sleeping bags

and bags of popcorn and flashlights.

They tiptoed across the yard

to the barn.

On the ladder Caroline Rose thought

she brushed against a spiderweb.

Ivy thought she heard a mouse squeak.

They laid out their sleeping bags.

They shined their flashlights.

But they could not see Hebby.

"We have to turn off

the flashlights," said Caroline Rose.

"Why?" asked Ivy.

"Because the spiders might see us."

Ivy opened her eyes wide.

"And don't eat the popcorn,"

said Caroline Rose.

"Why?" asked Ivy.

"If we let the mice eat it,"

said Caroline Rose,

"they will be too full to nibble

on our socks."

Ivy opened her eyes wider.

Just then something small and black swooped across the hayloft.

"EEEEEE!" screamed Ivy.

Then something big and striped leaped across the hay.

"AAAAAA!" yelled Caroline Rose.

They dived into their sleeping bags.

"Bats!" said Ivy from the bottom
of her sleeping bag. "Let's go."

"No!" said Caroline Rose
from the bottom of hers.

"Why not?" asked Ivy.

"If we get up," said Caroline Rose,
"the bats will make nests
in our hair."

"Ohhhhh!" cried Ivy.

"Don't worry," said Caroline Rose.

"Hebby will chase them away."

After a while Caroline Rose and Ivy

peeked out of their sleeping bags.

All they saw was hay.

All they heard was silence.

Suddenly another bat swooped!

Hebby leaped again!

Swoop! Leap! Swoop! Leap!

Finally Caroline Rose sat up

to count swoops and leaps.

Ivy sat up to eat popcorn.

All night they hopped in and out

of their sleeping bags.

They squealed and screamed.

They giggled and laughed.

At last the bats settled into the rafters.

Hebby made a nest in the hay.

Caroline Rose and Ivy yawned

and fell asleep in the hayloft

for the very first time.